ONCE UPON A FUTURE

ONCE UPON A FUTURE

Tales From the New World

Angela Young-Richie

To: Cheryl Henderson —

God's Love Always Prevails!

Angela Young-Richie

12-14-02

Writers Club Press

San Jose New York Lincoln Shanghai

Once Upon A Future
Tales From the New World

Writers Club Press
an imprint of iUniverse, Inc.

For information address:
iUniverse, Inc.
5220 S. 16th St., Suite 200
Lincoln, NE 68512
www.iuniverse.com

Author's Contact Information
Email: Gigiwrites@AOL.com

ISBN: 0-595-25028-9

Printed in the United States of America

To my loving husband, Curtis, and our "eggs", Marcus and Michelle.

CONTENTS

▼

STORY #1:
L.O.C.U.S.T.S.

My name is Dr. Loretta Rodgers. This tape-recorded message is a testimony that life has been forever altered. I am not sure what the future will bring, but I can tell you of my past and the present turmoil we all face......

I was a self-made woman. I had no time for men, marriage, or family. My research was all the relationship I needed. I was committed to that, and that only. Besides, I was so close to making the world a perfect and safe place. Surely that was more important than any ordinary existence.

For me, years of schooling and remaining focused on academic achievement had paid-off immensely. I was proud to be the first African American woman to receive a Bachelor Degree in Mechanical Engineering from Massachusetts Institute of Technology (M.I.T.) with a 4.0 grade point average every semester. Going on to complete my Master's in biophysics in just 14 short months was simply par for the course. My dual doctorate degrees from Cornell University in Robotic Engineering and Molecular Restructuring propelled me into the field of Cybernetic Engineering. I was profoundly capable of fusing studies in biological properties with electro-mechanical capabilities. My research and developments reshaped the field of Robotics and launched it well into the future. My current project would truly be the pinnacle of world research.

PAUSE—Loretta nervously cleared her throat and was forced to press the pause button. Emotionally overwhelmed with pangs of anxiety she well remembered once feeling her entire genius was uniquely woven into every aspect of project L.O.C.U.S.T.S. It was what she was born to create. She thought more tears would come, but even they were repressed. Loretta refocused, restarted the tape and proceeded to tell her story.....

Fourteen days ago I left my well secured suburban home, and took the 40 minute drive into work—giving me time to reflect on many things. I drove passed uniformed police posted along the road and on street corners. They were openingly sporting automatic weapons as deterrents to looters and robbers. Their military-like presence was designed to make the public feel safe and protected, but in actuality it was more for show than function. Stealing and looting took place on various levels in the United States as it struggled with shortages in goods and services in this New World order. This reality had become constant for every citizen. I could see it, and not see it happening all around me. I could drive into work, oblivious to what had become normal.

On that particular day, for seemingly no particular reason my thoughts drifted back to childhood years of being a "teachers' pet". Most of the kids in my classes hated me because I was so smart, and got most of the attention. My high level of intelligence continually made me different from all the other kids. That difference always equated into special treatment from educators—treatment I easily accepted and grew to expect. Being intellectually superior to others was never frightening. I just maintained lower expectations of everyone else. As early as kindergarten, I was given a battery of psychological and intelligence assessments. None of the tests presented even the slightest challenge. By the fifth grade I was passing assessments designed for senior high school students.

The testing served little purpose for my parents. They were strong, hard working people. They were proud of me just because I was their child. My father, a postal supervisor, and mother, an elementary school teacher, had no problem realizing that their daughter was a child prodigy. For them, it simply was the way God planned it. I was their only child, and possessed many gifts that attributed to my intelligence and abilities. A clear and reliable photographic memory, along with exceptional memory recall, and superior reasoning ability was all comprised in the little dynamo they lovingly called, "Retta."

Love, loving, lovingly! Why did the concept always present a problem? My parents were my parents. They did the best they could for me. I always understood that they felt this thing called "love" for me, but what is love, really? Is loving my job an appropriate feeling too? Is it okay to love my own interests and accomplishments, or just reserve this feeling for how I am affected by other people?

.......Still recounting the drive into work that morning, speaking clearly into the microphone, Loretta also remembered how her silent thoughts transformed into spoken words that day. It was then she mumbled displeasure with being a successful, 38-year old genius, in the year 2035, but still haunted by childhood experiences.

"What's love got to do with it, anyway?" Loretta stoically asked herself as she paused from taping. Not wanting to trail off from her mission at hand, she continued after just a moment to regroup. Pressing play, she resumed her taped account of the previous days' strange events.........

Errrrrrrrrr! "Oh sh**!" was my vocal response while slamming on the car brakes, just before nearly rear-ending the slow turning compact car in front of me. That was enough diversion to bring me back to the task at hand—driving my mint-condition, nostalgic 1999, midnight black, 2-seater BMW Z-3 safely to work. There was simply no replacing foreign cars nowadays. The near miss was certainly another reminder that love wasn't something for me to be concerned about. I believed that trying to figure out the love thing would only tie into all kinds of memories of my parents diligently trying to convince me that love was important, and that even God is love. Love and God just never made any sense. Why dig up all those old arguments anyway? Besides, I was just about to pull into the lab's entrance.

CHECK POINT ONE. The signs and electronic postings at Global Dynamics Laboratories were large, well lit, and impossible to miss. The organization wanted no misunderstandings. No excuses would ever be accepted for not adhering to the entrance procedures. If anyone ignored the obvious postings it was shoot first—ask questions later. I had well rehearsed the daily ritual of entering the research compound.

First, my vehicle was electronically scanned by overhead, under-carriage, and side view beams of ultraviolet light, designed to detect unauthorized devices like weapons or photographic instruments. Continuing a little more than 100 feet on the same single road of entry, I reached the guard post. It was always a three-person operation. To my knowledge, each guard had specific and varied tasks to perform. Alvin Ray was usually the one to speak to me and scan my ID badge. He was always jovial and full of pleasant greetings.

"Good morning, Dr. Rodgers. Looks like the rain will hold off for one more day. Not sure the flowers can wait though."

Most days I could handle the nice-a-tees and casual talk, but that day was an exception. I just wanted to get out of the car, into the lab, and settle down to work as quickly as possible. A bland "Hello, Mr. Ray," was the most I could squeeze out.

As an added precaution, Carl Williams painstakingly checked all automobile trunks, and confirmed vehicle models and license plate numbers. What a hassle if anyone drove a different car to work! There were mounds of red tape just to notify the authorities and security of the change. Last year one of my colleagues parked a borrowed car 3 blocks away in a public parking lot, and walked through the check-in process. That proved to be much less trouble!

Fred Walton dutifully confirmed clearance from Check Point One, and informed Check Point Two of my impending arrival. The curved and narrow single lane was approximately a half-mile ride. The grounds of Global Dynamics Laboratories were always immaculate. I believed such beauty provided excellent cover-up for the underground activities they cloaked. Nearly a hundred acres of land was blanketed with vibrant green grass and luscious flowering bushes strategically sewn throughout the mostly flat landscape. The most outstanding resident of this palatial view of nature was a century-old enormous bonsai tree. It proudly stood near the front entrance as a beacon drawing all attention to it. Normally the drive to Check Point Two provided just enough time for me to summarize how my workday would begin. That day none of my thoughts settled into place. Why in the world did I start reminiscing about my early school days, life with my parents, and all that crap! I had become an expert at repressing any feelings deemed non-productive. Why let them get in the way of my work? Just sometimes—sometimes, unresolved feelings surfaced in spite of my incredible self-control. I, Dr. Loretta Rodgers, liked being in charge. I liked knowing I controlled all aspects of my life. To maintain my successful and highly productive nature I only engaged in those activities and consciously harbored thoughts that fed my professional drive. I had to re-group quickly and prepare to give Project L.O.C.U.S.T.S. my undivided attention.

CHECK POINT TWO was a two-person security post. No actual contact with a guard was required. My vehicle was again electronically scanned. The guards monitored the scan and nodded their approval. As I proceeded my car was sprayed with an utltraviolent beam from an overhead device. This enhanced the vehicle scanning of photographic equipment, computer discs and any other possible "contraband" when I exited Global Dynamics at the end of the day.

The road led directly to the parking garage, now just 20 feet away. Surveillance cameras, bright lights around the clock, and security on foot patrol were standard. I felt valet parking would have been a perfect touch! Until that was available I was on my own to park in an assigned space.

CHECK POINT THREE. This Check Point had three entrances connecting the parking garage to the laboratory's main building. A simple swipe of my ID badge through a card reader was sufficient to gain entry.

Finally, my day could truly begin. Heading to my office first was just out of routine. Nothing in particular drew me there. It was largely a place to hang my coat and check e-mail messages. On the other hand, my co-workers offices' were sometimes hangouts, meeting rooms, and places to showcase family pictures and personal momentos. I had no need for all that. The lab was my refuge.

There was no getting around it. I had to pass Dr. Estrada's office to get to the main lab, my primary focus today. As anticipated, his ever-inclusive call bellowed the second I attempted to pass his doorway.

"Dr. Rodgers. Please join us for a morning cup of java. We're reviewing yesterday's testing."

I learned functional socializing while in college. To receive information and to have my input considered, I knew the importance of at least appearing interested in others. Nonetheless, I always felt that the team approach was often a hindrance to what I could produce on my own. I gave myself credit for knowing how and when to play the game.

The coffee was good, but the discussion was even better. The first two L.O.C.U.S.T.S. prototypes were confirmed a success! Night vision testing led by Drs. Kozloz, an immigrant from Russia, and Franklin, an African-American genius from the aerospace industry, produced results beyond what was predicted. Dr. Estrada, a native of Cuba, was the team leader and project coordinator, and probably the most insistent on the team approach of sharing—sharing failures and successes. I was never quite impressed with that approach, but learned to work within its framework. I was solely responsible for creating the cybernetic technology that gave life to the L.O.C.U.S.T.S., and wasn't about to share that fact indefinitely.

The U.S. military strength and morale at home and overseas had become weakened by government budget cuts, and historical indecisiveness over how or when to intervene in terrorists situations. With the United Nations recently defunct, the United States appeared segregated from the expanding power base now emerging from Italy, Russia, and portions of the Middle East. L.O.C.U.S.T.S.

would be a new trump card for the United States at home and abroad.

The Long-range Optical Combat Urgent and Surveillance Tactical Systems was designed to gather intelligence and to protect. They could be produced at a moderate cost, and required no human to be placed in physical danger. From anywhere in the world the activity of L.O.C.U.S.T.S. could be programmed and monitored. They were compact, with a twelve-inch long body, and two sets of wings. The forewings spanned a total of 24 inches. Their mechanical bodies were covered with synthetic biological material that would allow them to appear as large birds if detected by radar. In appearance, they resembled short-horned locusts.

The prototypes were capable of a flight speed of 170 miles per hour while in stealth-mode, cloaked from even the most sophisticated radar. A goal already in the works is for them to reach the speed of light. Synthetic-bio overlay material also enhanced the units' movements in flight and tolerance of environmental changes in temperature and altitude. The internal mechanical mechanisms were further protected by strong, flexible, artificial materials resembling the scales and hair of short-horned locusts. Tactical flight and maneuverability allowed L.O.C.U.S.T.S. to maintain flight indefinitely. They could hover in one distinct place, or relocate from point to point within a 170-mile single jolt. They never ate, slept, or complained. They would become the new army.

Their 360-degree rotating optical scopes were positioned behind two large portals that resembled human eyes. Sonic receptor implants along both sides of the L.O.C.U.S.T.S.' abdomen recorded and interpreted sounds from the environment. What they saw and heard would be transmitted back to a home base for human observers to witness.

Their longer hind set of legs allowed them to hop at high altitudes, jumping with ease from the ground to a tree and back again. They scaled walls quickly and orderly, maneuvering like trained commandos—never breaking rank, never crowding each other.

Their shorter front legs also served as grips. They could grab or claw objects and people with tremendous force. Thousands of long, thin tentacles of hair covered their bodies. Each long hair was an antenna. Working in unison the hairs created a continuos receptive force, a sense of touch analyzing its environment. This force enabled a type of radar to detect aggressive forces like air or ground assault missiles, and other weaponry. L.O.C.U.S.T.S. possessed two major weapons: long, sharp teeth of galvanized steel, and a thirty-inch projectile tail. The tail emanated stinging laser beams. The beams could be set to simply stun a victim, or produce deadly results. Humans safely operating from a home base could program and control L.O.C.U.S.T.S.

At first glance some may say they were grotesque. However, L.O.C.U.S.T.S. were designed for their ability to function and for their longevity. There was beauty in the work they could perform. The implications for their use in national and international security were endless.

Discussion about the recent success had elevated to vocal elation and bold cheers. Leaving Dr. Estrada's office now would not be wise. Key scientists, their lab assistants, and even a few secretaries had been drawn into the hoopla. I had no idea where the champagne came from, but it was suddenly there in full force, replacing the morning coffee.

Truly, the champagne wasn't the only substance bubbling. My blood began to boil and bubble too. There was still additional testing to perform. I was ready to press-on. For me this celebration was premature and just not necessary. I wanted to see the L.O.C.U.S.T.S. in full operation. I wanted to see them instill the order and control they were designed to produce before we declared the project a complete success. For now, I needed to smile and cheer and play the game. Timing was everything. I had to look the part of a team member. I played my part well.

The celebration lasted most of the morning. Yet, the workday seemed to drag on. In the lab it was difficult for everyone to settle into the next phase of testing. Was it the champagne, or knowing that decades of work had produced two fully operative L.O.C.U.S.T.S.? Secretly I could feel the excitement raging in my soul. This was probably as close as I would ever get to giving birth. For me, this was close enough.

I managed to work 4 hours, setting-up a test to check wing and flight correction sequences which could be activated when a wing became damaged from environmental elements, or attacks. The computer program associated with the test would run through the sequence for the remainder of the workday and all night. It was about 3:30 PM. I decided to head home early for a change. To me it seemed that somehow I had let my guard down. My morning drive into work and the day's excitement had taken its toll. Concentration was out of the question. I took one long look at my winged "babies" and called it a day.

Traveling through the Check Points in reverse and exiting Global Dynamics produced a sigh of relief. The project I was instrumental in creating had reached a successful stage. The United States would take back its controlling position in the world, and become a force to be reckoned with. My fellow scientists and I truly believed that world peace could only be achieved if dominated by the military intelligence from this part of the world.

That day exiting Global Dynamics was a complete pleasure for me. At the end of most other days I would anxiously think of what would be my first task when returning to the lab. That day only escape was on my mind.

In no time at all I was driving along and listening to the late afternoon news on the car radio. I would not allow the 40-minute ride home to be a repeat of the ride into work. The radio was a good deterrent. The news stories were typical. Internationally, unrest in the Middle East was continuing with full force. According to the latest reports the Russian Prime Minister's leadership of the invasion into Middle East four years ago created unity for some, but disparity for others. Civilian and military forces continued to be divided along religious and ethnic lines. The recent car bombing in Israel was another terrorist attack aimed at discouraging religious expression.

To me this was further proof of America's need to gain back world dominance. It took the time of generations, but America finally grew non-judgmental of individuals abilities based on race, ethnicity and gender criteria. Differences in skin color had ceased to be a measurement of one's worth. Terms like prejudice and racism had finally lost their zeal. However, elsewhere on the planet, division among people remained paramount. The unrest in the Middle East was as old as time itself. Someone has to step in to claim order and equity for all.

Due to American stock market crashes and unscrupulous business tactics on non-American soil, the center of world power and commerce had firmly shifted from the United States of America to Rome, Italy. Rome became a strong and constant ally of Russia and China, nearly ostracizing the United States of America. Technology made Italy and her allies strong in areas of military might, manufacturing, and communication. Together the allies were able to produce what ever they needed to survive. Rome maintained formal relations with Great Britain, but only to keep a close eye on them and to enjoy the import of theatre and premium tea blends.

Our loss of control and impact in the world market was the catalyst for patriotism and a new sense of nationalism in The United States. No one else in the world needed us, except us. We returned to growing most of our own food, and relied primarily on resources found in North America. Bartering with our South American neighbors proved necessary for the acquisition of some textiles and food crops. Luxury items like designer clothing, perfumes, and most foreign cars became high premiums for some and far less of a need for others. The ability to purchase any luxury item certainly magnified the line between the "haves" and "have-nots". Periodic shortages in food and energy sources were apparent, yet most had adapted.

Nonetheless, we were still effected and influenced by what happened in Europe and elsewhere. Whose to say the return of racism and separatism still prevalent in other parts of the world wouldn't take a strong hold in the West, again? With greatly reduced import and export trade in the U.S.A., the ever-apparent shortages of goods and services, downsizing and corporate reorganization could do strange and desperate things to people. If our newfound sense of nationalism did not prevail would we revert socially?

Rome hadn't possessed world domination since ancient biblical time, and yet some of the same ancient problems amiably survived. Even with Rome as a supporter, does the Russian Prime Minister really believe he'll get away with his attack on the Middle East? Who will stop him? L.O.C.U.S.T.S. would be the answer to the world's continued need to ensure peaceful co-existence among all people. They would monitor all activities and protect against insurrection.

Just like a well-rehearsed ritual, my thoughts shifted from changing the world to the task now at hand—pulling into the entrance of my condo community. Observing the security officers at the entrance gate and preparing to punch in my ID code on the key pad, I once again justified the importance of my life's work. My

L.O.C.U.S.T.S. would make it possible for everyone to live safe and productive lives; not only government scientists like myself.

Finally, I reached the entrance to my condominium. I was in full view of the familiar sight of small well-manicured lawns that seemed to envelop each 2-bedroom unit. Every unit had forsythia bushes carefully planted at the corners of each property, and a limited variety of annuals meticulously placed in flower boxes, or lined along narrow walkways. Early spring days like today found each small lawn ablaze with forsythia blossoms. The landscape was painted with their brilliant yellow flowers, radiating across the land just as the noonday sun illuminates the sky. In a much more subdued manner, only a few oak trees dotted the scenery.

There was very little variation in the architecture of each split-level unit in the 54-condominium complex. From any sidewalk, facing any condo, the same style large bay window at the left front corner of the house looked down on a small concrete porch. Next to the bay window, a pine front door was carefully stained a redwood tone, and trimmed with tiny non-descript carvings intended to be decorative, but easily overlooked. A pair of standard windows was positioned side by side and right of the front door. A single car garage was attached to the right side of the house, appearing snapped on much like a child connects legos. The houses were simplistic, basic, and most of all in a safe area. A constant band of armed security personnel patrolled through the community. Sight of them was an affective deterrent to would-be attackers, or thieves. An unattractive electrical fence wrapped around the entire complex and served as a source of electrocution of brawlers, as well as a surveillance belt, housing several cameras overseeing everyone's movements. Surveillance cameras were also strategically placed in trees or on street light poles. Somewhere, someone was watching and protecting. None of this appeared aesthetically tasteful, but personal security was the beauty my neighbors and I grew to admire.

With my prized BMW Z-3 safely tucked away I entered my home. I was ready for a world of peace, quiet, and relaxation—until I heard Dorothy Knox's familiar spiritual crooning. *"....Lord, help me to hold out—until my cha-a-n-ge comes!"*

I slammed the door connecting the garage and the kitchen to announce my arrival. The singing stopped and Dorothy appeared.

"Well, hello Dr. Retta. I'm usually finished with the housework before you get home. What a pleasure it is to see you!"

"Hello Miss Dorothy." I managed to get myself together and calmly glided through the immaculate little kitchen to reach my small and sparsely furnished dining room. I quickly determined that the dining room would be the least comfortable place, surely discouraging prolonged conversation.

"I decided to leave a little early today. It's been a hectic day."

As predicted, Dorothy followed on my heels.

"Lord, child! You're still the spit'in image of your mother standing there looking so pretty." Dorothy was honestly overcome with nostalgia as she hastily continued. "I tell you, your mother was the best friend I ever had. When you were a little thing growing up, I was just a young mother on the block, and didn't know much about noth'in. You're mother......."

"Miss Dorothy!" My interruption nearly startled the older women. Silence fell between us. Suddenly eye-to-eye contact alone sufficiently replaced all verbalizations. After a moment's thoughtful gaze, with unruffled composure Dorothy broke the silence.

"Well, Dr. Retta. I don't mean to go on and on about the past. I can see you're ready to settle in for the evening."

"Yes. Thank-you." My mechanical politeness brought immediate closure to our exchange. Not expecting a response, Dorothy extended her usual affirmation as she departed through the front door.

"God is good Dr. Retta. All we have to do is trust in him."

GOOD! GOOD! What goodness? Now on my own turf and safely secluded, my emotions exploded into shouts of disbelief and extreme anger. Still standing in the tiny dining room, with arms flailing and feet pounding down on the floorboards, my past gushed out before me as if kayaking on wild water rapids. What goodness could have possibly been found in the automobile accident death of my father 12 years ago? The stress of coping with the loss drove my mother to heart failure and the grave just about a year after dad's death.

I went on to growl about the lack of goodness in the loss of food crops, production of basic household supplies, inconsistent availability of heating oil, or frequent interruptions in electrical service for the general population. These situations had led to despair, countless attacks on innocent people, and periodic rioting. Stepped-up police patrols and National Guard intervention had not been enough to command optimum control. Scientists, agriculturist, and civic engineers were hard at work developing plans and methods to restore some of the abundance of life we knew before the base of world power shifted from the U.S.A. to Europe. As if standing before a congressional audience, I passionately declared my fear for the nation if its citizens succumbed to chaos. Anarchy would surely prevail. Restoration of our American culture would be impossible. My final outburst summarized everything. "If God is so good and full of love, why does he let bad things happen to good people?"

It was over. No more shouting. No more waving of arms and balling up of fists. No more heavy pacing. I had cleansed my heart and soul. Dorothy's biblical words of encouragement had long since fallen on death ears. I would continue to trust in no one but myself—my own power, my own abilities. The only goodness I could believe in now was L.O.C.U.S.T.S.

Sleep came easily. Perhaps due to my overall exhaustion, or a sense of freedom gained from the emotional release. Whatever the reason, I awoke refreshed and ready for the world. My mind was strong and in sync with my conscious goals. An exhilarating shower, simple breakfast of toast, fruit, and orange juice, comfortable clothes concealed by a lab coat, and I was more than ready to start the workday. I was back on track.

My usual, nonchalant wave to the security guard at the condominium's only entrance was just one more small indication that normalcy was recaptured. I figured it was best to forget all about yesterday's undesired occurrences. I wondered how the L.O.C.U.S.T.S. wing and flight correction testing concluded. That would be the first thing I checked.

The drive into work was going along as expected. The usual police patrols were evident. Vacant storefronts dotted the once vivarant local shopping centers. Some buildings had been re-opened and used as government sponsored emergency food distribution centers. Many storeowners who were able to remain in business did not allow customers in their establishments. With the aide of built-in turn-styles, orders were taken through bulletproof glass windows. This required the customer to remain out on the sidewalk, and the merchant safely inside from probable harm.

I rode by what seemed to be 4 police officers questioning a middle age poorly dressed couple on foot. Both had large packages in their arms. I figured they were being questioned for possible theft of some sort. From what I could quickly gather the man was nervously boisterous and rapidly shook his head. I was convinced it would be a desperate situation for all parties involved. As usual, the police probably didn't actually see the man or woman take anything, but the couple's large bundles just made them look suspicious. They could have a perfectly legitimate explanation, but be nervous, and that alone would make them suspect. It could be logged in at police headquarters as a routine pedestrian stop, or end up a full-fledged arrest. It could go either way.

Continuing the drive to work, I was reminded that traffic was never too heavy. Few people had access to, or the money for gasoline—let alone a car. Bicycle riders and pedestrians were more the norm. Everything looked as it should.

Suddenly, an extreme burst of what seemed like light flashed all around me. For just a moment my vision was completely impaired. My eyes were wide open, yet a colorless brightness coated everything I thought I should be able to see. In that instance all sounds were completely muted. There was no time to react. My eyes remained fixed in front of me attempting to peer through the windshield. My foot remained on the accelerator, pressing down as before. My hands gripped the steering wheel. I was just about to turn left onto Freedman Boulevard.

Just as suddenly, the blinding, colorless illumination disappeared. I was still pressing down on the accelerator and consequently slammed into the rear of the police cruiser that had been safely ahead of me only a moment ago. The swift jolt caused the air bag to deploy. My head was forced back and smacked against the doorframe. I screamed from agony and fear, but my reflexes were not dulled. I pushed the inflated air bag aside and opened the car door almost simultaneously. My heart beat crazily, signifying a violent adrenaline rush. I was convinced that as long as I was conscious I would be in control. Nonetheless, my movements were awkward. I climbed out of the car like a drunken partygoer tackling a flight a stairs. I grabbed my head and tried to push back the blood that mixed in my once neatly cropped hair, and began to run down the left side of my face blurring my vision. I slowly became aware of the screams and helpless wailing of others, but was unable to completely focus on my immediate surroundings. From my lab coat pocket I removed an old scarf and wiped some blood from my face. I then used the scarf as a makeshift tourniquet around my head. The pain was throbbing, rhythmic like a persistent leaky faucet. It seemed like an hour had passed, but only a few minutes actually ticked by before clear sight was restored.

I could see the unexplainable wreckage of cars driven up on sidewalks or slammed into buildings, engines still running. Bikes once upright and mobile were now discarded by their owners and laid horizontally on the street. Mysterious piles of clothes remained where it seemed people had been walking or riding by.

A man ran by yelling, "What's going on! Where did everybody go!"

He grabbed me by the shoulders and attempted to shake answers out of me. Self-preservation and shock made it easy to push the demented man aside. He stumbled like a zombie down the main road in search of someone else to question.

Where *did* everyone go? I quietly panicked, but looked around in every direction. I saw more of the same—cars without drivers, bicycles abandoned, and piles of clothes and shoes where pedestrians should have been. Only a few people remained on the once busy street. All were dazed and searching for answers. Had the city been bomb?

I felt confident I'd find solace in the lab. I was still six miles away. Driving would be the quickest way, but my car was no longer operable. On the other side of the road I spotted a car without a driver, engine still running, and only slightly pulled up on the curb. It looked as if it could be driven. Before getting seated I threw out a man's suit, shirt, tie, and underwear—all piled in the drivers seat as if their owner simply melted away. His shoes and socks were left propped against the accelerator and brake pedals ready for his next move. Those too I quickly grabbed and threw down to the ground.

Where was everybody? What happened? These questions became repetitive like the throbbing in my head. Answers would be found at the lab.

The drive was horrendous. The few people I did see were stunned and visibly full of fear. I drove through an obstacle course of crashed cars and motionless bicycles. Less than ½ mile from the lab I heard an unusual roaring sound. Was it a squadron of helicopters, or low flying stealth bombers? Whatever it was, it was coming closer, and from the sky.

I pulled the car off the main street and parked behind a small group of abandoned stores, nearly wedging the car between two corroded dumpsters. Then I saw them. Their wings flapped in unison. Their eyes were open and alert. Their tails were partially protracted.

L.O.C.U.S.T.S., too numerous to count, too alive to be pro-grammed by anyone. As they flew overhead they sounded more like thunder, and appeared to be an enormous storm cloud, blotting out the sun's rays. Fear gripped my very being. I could feel the evidence of physical shock beginning at the top of my head with a warm sen-sation, then it gravitated down through my body like a wave of hor-izontal nerve endings. How could this be? Where did they all come from? I had only made two. How did they multiply?

Numb and without emotion, I got out of the car. I walked out into the open. People were running through the streets and back driveways. Some L.O.C.U.S.T.S. flew lower and zapped their human prey with rays from their extended tails. The wailing and cries from the tortured people were agonizing. The L.O.C.U.S.T.S seemed to be testing their capabilities. Stinging some frightened people, and terrorizing others by biting them. Some people were grabbed by one arm and lifted a few feet off the ground only to be dropped without warning. The horrified people were maimed and bled through their clothing, but no one was killed. L.O.C.U.S.T.S. scaled buildings and broke through windows in search of more vic-tims.

On foot, scurrying through driveways and side streets, I made my way to the grounds of Global Dynamics Laboratories. The land-scape was immaculate as usual. Everything looked peaceful. All was quiet. No one and nothing was stirring.

I approached CHECKPOINT ONE to find the maintenance crew's van with its engine loudly churning, and left in the parking gear. Peering in I saw two piles of blue uniforms draped by outer jackets and topped with baseball-style caps donned with the company logo. I frantically ran into the guards' glass enclosed booth, but there was no sign of Alvin Ray, Carl Williams, or Fred Walton. Only their uniforms and name badges remained in three identical bundles.

Physical fatigue from the morning's events began to overtake me and caused me to swagger along down the familiar path leading to CHECKPOINT TWO. Seeing piles of clothing and shoes behind this glass enclosed booth mimicked a familiar sight. Nonetheless, I looked around bewildered. The air was motionless. The usual sounds of birds chirping, and the early morning ringing echoes of crickets were absent from this scene. I could only hear distant cries of people being attacked by *my* L.O.C.U.S.T.S. I had to get into the lab. I had to find out what went wrong.

By the time I reached CHECKPOINT THREE I became light-headed and felt faint. There was no need to swipe my ID badge through the card reader. All of the entrance doors were wide open. Without encountering anyone I walked onto the ground level corridor. This particular corridor wrapped around onto the first floor of the building. I planned to take the elevator leading to the main laboratory housed on the second floor. My trek to the elevator was littered with ripped papers, broken beakers and flasks, and office furniture tossed about. Yet, no one was stirring. I cautiously walked passed Dr. Estrada's office, and the offices of my other colleagues. Their doors were closed, and the offices dark as if no one had arrived to start the day. Perhaps they were stuck on the road, or worse yet, attacked by L.O.C.U.S.T.S. Maybe they too disappeared, leaving only a pile of clothing?

I rode the elevator without incident. The doors opened to silence and evidence of more destruction. I proceeded with caution and dismay. Just as I turned the corridor to reach the main lab I spotted Bernadette Matthews, the project's senior lab assistant. She was crouched down in a corner, obviously frightened, and frantically trying to strike a match to light a cigarette. Her fingers glistened from teardrops, and her hands shook wildly. Her task seemed impossible. We startled each other as we became equally aware of our shared presence. Yet, somehow seeing another human being was immediate comfort, and eliminated the reaction to flee.

At that moment I saw a very different Bernadette Matthews. Bernadette was usually loud spoken, consistently overbearing, and spewed confidence even when she was wrong. Bernadette had a way of improvising on specific directions. She frequently, independently instituted changes to procedures. Even though her changes turned out to be appropriate and implemented at the right time, problems arose when Bernadette did not inform others of the changes she made. Too often her methods of monitoring tests did not coincide with what others had previously decided on, and as a result data was sometimes not stored or not interpreted properly. I had had my share of run-ins with Bernadette. It was safe to say we did not like each other. Without emotion, we silently maintained eye contact as I sluggishly walked over to her. It was nearly all I could do to simply slide down the wall, and crouch next to the only person around who may be able to communicate something about this morning's calamity.

Exhaustion had taken its toll. I had just enough energy to remove the matches from Bernadette's moist trembling hands, strike one, and attempt to light the cigarette for her. The cigarette moved erratically like an out of control cursor on a computer monitor, but I accomplished the task. When it was finally lit I stretched out my weak legs, leaned my sore back against the wall, and gave a deep sigh of relief. I listened as Bernadette gave an account of what happened.

Bernadette talked about her arrival to the lab as "business as usual". It was midnight Tuesday. She worked third shift this week. Bernadette looked in on the L.O.C.U.S.T.S. at about 12:30. They were fine. She knew the wing and flight correction sequences would run independently. She didn't have time to bother with the testing anyway. She planned on catching up on program coding for surveillance maneuvers that would be re-tested later in the week. Few people were around on the third shift. No one was in her way. All night it was quiet, deadly quiet. Only a few maintenance personnel, a handful of security guards, and 1 secretary putting in overtime to transcribe Dr. Franklin's lab notes were in the building.

Just before 7:30 AM Bernadette decided to look in on the L.O.C.U.S.T.S. one last time before going home. As she approached the lab she could hear glass breaking. Two security guards hurriedly approached from the opposite direction. Bernadette became glassy eyed and stared blankly as she described how one second the guards were there, and the next second she only saw their clothing in 2 separate piles on the floor. They just disappeared into thin air.

Bernadette took a long speechless pause. I feared she was going to stop there. She began fumbling in her pocket and eventually retrieved a nearly crushed pack of cigarettes. I quietly observed. This time she independently lit another one. After a long and thoughtful drag of tobacco Bernadette continued where she left off.

She talked of confusion and uncertainty in remembering how the lab door opened. She couldn't determine if she had been brave enough to open it herself. Did the L.O.C.U.S.T.S. manipulate the retina-coded security entry and exit procedure? She could only clearly remember standing at the open door and looking in at them—all of them. They were on the walls, the ceiling, and sprinting throughout the laboratory.

Once the door opened, L.O.C.U.S.T.S. hopped or flew out at will. Breaking momentarily from her narrative, Bernadette starred down at her bruised legs and reminisced of how she fell down on her knees to duck away from the grand exodus. As the L.O.C.U.S.T.S. escaped she was knocked over. Her hair was pulled. L.O.C.U.S.T.S. bit and scratched her. She was petrified.

Natural reflexes took over and Bernadette wrapped her arms around her head and curled up like a ball. The attack ended as quickly as it started. When she peered out between folded arms she saw the two original L.O.C.U.S.T.S. unstrapped from the table that served as their resting-place during the wing and flight correction sequence testing. Like all the others, these two had become so very alive. Their mechanical nature had evolved into a complete life force. They exhibited an aura of power and purpose. A purpose not controlled by mere human beings.

The pair looked at Bernadette with utter disgust as they hopped towards her. Sharp metal teeth clanged anxiously in their vicious mouths. Their tails became distended, ready to attack with stinging, deadly laser rays. To run away would have been futile. Bernadette was stunned by their show of power. She was paralyzed. How did they multiply? Who or what controlled them?

The voice of her grandmother suddenly moved through her head. Bernadette heard one of her frequent bible quotes—something she called a psalm—psalm 46:1-2. Bernadette watched death approach as her grandmother's memory whispered, "*God is our refuge and strength, a very present help in trouble. Therefore we will not fear, though the earth should change.*" The L.O.C.U.S.T.S. hovered over Bernadette. The drone of their wings revved up like engines in flight. Instead of attacking her, they flew away with great speed.

Bernadette sat up straight and surveyed the aftermath of terror and destruction so evident in the lab. Somehow she pulled to her feet and hobbled out. She could only assume she some how crawled out of the lab and collapsed at the corner where I found her.

After hearing Bernadette's story one revelation consumed my thoughts. I had to find that book. I hadn't read anything in it for years, nor had I ever embraced its teachings. But, I couldn't help comparing what I had already seen the L.O.C.U.S.T.S. do, with the restraint they employed after hearing a quote from the bible. Could the answers be in that book? I knew that a few maintenance workers and security guards sometimes met over their bibles and talked about God during lunch-breaks. I remembered overhearing their urgent conversations about something called the Rapture. They said the Rapture would be a single, sudden event when Jesus the Christ would return and take his believers—his church—away from harm. They always seemed so happy about the whole thing. They talked of a *new* heaven and a *new* earth. They talked of being at peace with Jesus for an eternity. I had to find out more.

Cautiously I glided down the hallway, taking a speechless and apprehensive Bernadette with me. All was quiet. Most offices were still dark, waiting for their inhabitants to arrive for work. We were alone in the building. Our fear was being replaced with determination. We both agreed—we had to find that book.

At the other end of the hall, down from the main laboratory, I burst into the second floor maintenance office. Bernadette followed behind me, now a constant silent partner. The office was unscathed. We would be the ones to create destruction and mishap as we anxiously searched through desks and shelves. We haphazardly tossed aside manuals, pamphlets, and anything else that did not fit the description of a bible. Finally, neatly stacked in a bottom desk drawer I found not one, but two of the ancient books. I trembled with excitement and anticipation.

We grabbed the bibles and headed for the nearest exit. We couldn't take a chance on the L.O.C.U.S.T.S. possibly returning. Fatigue gripped our very souls, but we had to press on. We were no longer rivals. We were bound by our circumstance and neither wanted to be alone. Unceremoniously, we each kept a firm grasp on the bibles that had become our property—our source for salvation. Seemingly with renewed strength we left the building to secure a safe place. A place to hide from the L.O.C.U.S.T.S. A place to glean answers from the ancient books.

—END OF TAPING—

STORY #2:
DEBTORS LAMENT

We never knew picking peaches could be such an arduous task. How could something so abundant, juicy, and ripe take so much backbreaking work to gather! How many more thousands of bushels must we pick? We never knew how dirty we'd get doing this job. Coveralls and work gloves just didn't make a difference.

Why didn't they give us an inside job, doing work we could relate to? Carther was a computer programmer. I was teaching business computer software. Why didn't they just let us work in the computer chip factory? We never knew our predicament would get so bad. We just never knew.

"Annie, Annie."

I heard Carther calling me from a nearby row of trees. He must have been at the top level of his elevator platform. Sounded like he called me clear up from the clouds, but I heard the weakness in his voice too.

"What's wrong, Cart?"

"My arms and fingers are numb, Annie. I just can't reach for another one."

That's when I dropped the peaches from my hands, careful to make sure they landed in my basket. I hoped and prayed no one would steal from my count. But I couldn't worry about that. I didn't expect anyone to help us. Everyone was cautious of leaving their assigned posts. No one wanted to be marked for correction.

No one talked to each other much anyway. Sometimes couples like Cart and I didn't even talk to each other. I'm glad we were different. We still really cared about each other. I did my best to get to him quickly and without being noticed right away. At nearly 62 years of age I was still rather agile. Modern medicine and high potency vitamin injections kept most of us working full-time until age 82.

By the time I got to Carther's tree, Bill Shacker was there too. Wouldn't you know it! He noticed almost everything. Thank God, Bill was one of the more friendly and concerned Overseers. I could probably count on him to help us out, instead of mark us for a correction for an unscheduled work stoppage.

"Why ain't you at your tree, Annie?"

"Something's wrong with Carther, Mr. Shacker. I'm going to check on him."

We both found Cart leaning against his tree, but somehow still perched up on his elevator platform, forty-five feet above the ground. Bill Shacker radioed for a medical unit. They came in lightning speed. Bill Shacker had to put Cart's mechanical platform into a slow reverse to start his descent from the enormous peach tree. Cart had managed to hook his arms around the poles of the vertical conveyor. He clung for dear life, resembling a snail as he descended to safety. Before Cart neared the ground I could see that his deep rich brown color had become pale and muted. He felt so very cold and clammy.

"I love you, Annie. I'm sorry we got in this mess."

That's all he said before he passed out. He was still breathing. Thank God he was still breathing!

They whisked him away to the medical center. I was ordered back to my assigned post. The overseers told me I could see Carther when my workday was over. I obeyed. I returned to my tree. I could feel all eyes on me. Silence followed me back to my post. My basket was untouched. Strangely, that was so very comforting. I found solace in seeing that no one took advantage of our situation. No one stole our peaches for their own count.

I went back to picking. The sun was strong. The air was scented with the sweet fragrance of peaches—peaches, and more peaches. I became so full of emotion...fearful for Carther...angry about the limitations I was forced to accept...and sad that we ended up in this place. We just never knew that our credit card debt would land us in such deep trouble.

*   *   *   *

"HAPPY NEW YEAR!" Whistles were blowing. Party horns were tooting. Our small cozy house was converted into a miniature Time Square, New Year's Eve celebration. It had taken Carther about an hour to rig-up a basketball size mirrored ball—just like the one that used to be in Time Square up until the late 1980's. He was nostalgic that way. Cart took great pride in holding on to older ways of doing things. He just never accepted the electronic ball everyone else seemed to think was better just because it used modern technology.

We celebrated with a handful of longtime, close friends, but our enthusiasm was great. Like most of our friends, Cart and I were professionals in our fifties. We had seen, and in some cases helped to develop change in the world. Each one felt we had lots of time to handle even more. I felt like the world surrounded us as we counted down to the New Year. We were all happy and equally full of wonderment, just like young children on Christmas morning. We had waited a lifetime for the first minute of the first day, of the very first year of the Greater World Council (GWC). It was now 2020, and change felt good.

The GWC was inevitable. Several major events from the last quarter of the 20th century helped to make its creation possible. We thought we understood the changes. Basic human rights had become an absolute for everyone, everywhere. All people were safe and protected. All people ate nourishing food. Good housing, healthcare, and education became everyone's right worldwide.

These factors alone leveled the playing field. The economics of racism lost its fuel. No one had an advantage over anyone else. No one could assume an advantage based on skin color, ethnic background, age, or gender. There was no room or tolerance for terms like, "birth-right". Equality had been affected.

Everyone had a job, and was expected to participate in the well being and maintenance of their region. Collectively, the regions of the world governed and supported the Greater World Council. "Peace on earth," and "Goodwill to all" became more than mere words. They became our new reality. Humankind had really achieved utopia this time.

$$* \qquad * \qquad * \qquad *$$

At breaktime I quickly looked for Bill Shacker. Lord knows I was hungry and thirsty too, but I needed to know about Carther first. Most pickers coming down from their trees looked at me sadly. Some shook their heads. A few patted me on my shoulders when they scurried by. But it was Overseer Ruth Peterman's deep, bone chilling call that broke my stride. I turned and watched the six feet, five inch, Amazon-like woman approach me with such a slow monstrous gait. She had to be 30 years my junior, but always appeared sluggish and uncoordinated. We all knew that her bellowing, or threats to give marks for correction would reach us long before her physical presence. Standing my face to her enormous bosom, Overseer Peterman looked down at me and blurted out that Carther was stabilized, and evidently had suffered some level of cardiac arrest.

She smirked and reminded me that I could visit him in the medical center at the end of the workday. I wondered how much it would hurt her to care a little, just a little bit. At any rate, I was happy to hear some news. I wanted it to be positive, but what did "stabilize" really mean? Would Cart's condition worsen, or get better? If I could be by his side, comfort him, would that help to improve his condition?

*   *   *   *

The second day of the New Year Carther came home early from the bank. I was still on my holiday break from teaching, and our children weren't coming to visit until next week. I suppose its fair to say that everyone on the globe wanted to see the transmission first hand. As a bank employee, Cart felt his position might become obsolete. As a teacher of business computer software, I wasn't certain how my skills would be utilized in this New World Order. We still had mounting credit card bills, and loans to pay off. Throughout the years, using credit and borrowing money was how we made ends meet. We weren't extravagant in our spending, but we never seemed to have enough cash money to meet the needs and reasonable desires of our family. We did the best we could to get three children through the expenses of childhood, including education, extra curricular activities, orthodontic braces, and later college. We maintained up keep of our small, but comfortable home. We took modest vacations. We needed our jobs to pay our bills. We still had current expenses and past debts to pay-off. We were like so many other Americans. We had two cars, three times as many credit cards, and people respected us. We believed we had secured some level of middle-class status.

Cart and I were firmly perched in front of our video stage a full ten minutes before the Greater World Council began its simultaneous broadcast to the entire world. The VS was probably the most welcomed new age home entertainment device Cart ever used. Most affordable models had a rectangular platform, approximately 5 feet long and only 2 inches high. Most folks placed them against a plain white wall for optimal viewing clarity. The nearly life-size, three-dimensional images projected up from the VS platform provided a delightful, almost hypnotizing effect for the viewer. Clear, full, crisp color, and depth of images became a must in every home by 2010. Prior to video stages we had digital television. That basic digital technology experienced a short life span, much like that of the mini CD's of the 1980's! With VS, simply watching television evolved into witnessing events. This new technology utilized isolated telepathic selection. Headgear wasn't even necessary. After referring to a computerized VS Guide, we determined the date and time of a transmission we wanted to see, and simply pressed a thumb against the on/off scan pad, while "thinking" of our choice. Removal of the thumb locked in the selection, and the transmission remained visual until it ended, or until we telepathically cut it off by again using the on/off scan pad. For those who needed it, voice activated models were also available. In either case, brain waves made the connection to a central transmitting location, which then "bounced back" our desired program.

One representative from every continent spoke. We observed a rainbow of people describe an array of events. They started with a history—the basic background for the GWC's inception.

We were told how the world was lead to believe that AIDS (Acquired Immune Deficiency syndrome) was accidentally started in Africa during the development of an experimental polio vaccine. It was in the late 1950's when the people of Zaire were desperately battling another outbreak of paralytic polio. They were thankful to become one of the first groups to receive the vaccine. It was developed from a weakened form of the poliovirus grown in a culture of green monkey kidney cells. Actually, that anxiously awaited vaccine wasn't the only substance being tested, and administered to the inhabitants of the Congo. A second isolated group also living along equatorial Africa became "guinea pigs" for an entirely different purpose.

The Greater World council showed documentation that scientists and military personnel representing the United States, Great Britain, and Australia were jointly engaged in the search and development of a biological, non-airborne substance that could be used as a form of chemical warfare. The objective was to create a controlled substance that could specifically effect designated subjects. These scientists also experimented with tissue cultures from green monkeys—a species that carried a virus much like HIV (Human Immundeficiency Virus). Unwitting participants became incubators for the birth of acquired immune deficiency syndrome, commonly called AIDS.

Apparently, after testing along the Congo region, certain Middle East radical groups were then targeted as recipients of the virus. However, by the time the slow killing virus was determined too difficult to isolate and control, human nature had taken over, and HIV became a primarily sexually transmitted disease, preceding the deadly condition, AIDS. It struck both "desirables" and "undesirables" alike, all over the world.

The GWC representatives explained how the New World order would forever prevent such inhuman and threatening behavior. They used the former Union of Soviet Socialist Republics as an example of how the breakdown of a nation created chaos and violence for the newly forming nations. Back then, military control and domination became methods of survival. Now, we need only see ourselves as one entity—the human entity in a shared world. Respect and safety for all people.

Leaders from India and Pakistan jointly discussed how both countries rushed to develop nuclear weapons. We were reminded that in 1998, Pakistan proudly and arrogantly announced that they too possessed a nuclear weapon, just like their neighbor, India. At that time both nations were still greatly poverty stricken and volatile. Yet, they displayed their nuclear capabilities like two competitive schoolboys in a recess yard. The two leaders confirmed that under the past rule of India and Pakistan, the unavoidable human traits of greed, competition, power, and jealousy could have easily lead to nuclear war, and the destruction of the entire globe.

Now that the world had become so very advanced and connected economically and technologically, it was simply time to usher in a new era—The Greater World Council. Again, we were told how the GWC made way for consistent and equal government, and peace for the entire world. It all seemed to make good sense.

A panel of doctors and other medical professionals were up next. They reviewed how socialized medicine in one form or another had already been adopted throughout the globe by the year 2002. Now in place of HMO's, PPO's, and government-sponsored healthcare, every inhabitant of the world would be in the World Health Network. The professionals proudly announced that good and equitable healthcare was now an automatic human right.

One precocious looking physician pounded his fist on the conference table when he announced, "Gone were the days when a doctor was no longer the primary decision maker regarding which tests a patient would receive, or the length of a hospital stay."

Carther cheered too when this same doctor voiced his disgust that healthcare options had become controlled by business school graduates. Graduates that were hired to keep HMO cost down, and HMO owner's income up.

Carther always said having a business management person making healthcare decisions just didn't mix. Afterall, those business administrators would naturally be interested in the "bottom line." To give them the power to determine methods of healthcare and cure was truly ludicrous. An M.B.A., or any other business school graduate never took the Hippocratic Oath. They never dedicated their lives to do as much as possible to cure, and save lives. As African Americans, having to deal with a history of mistrust of any establishment, Cart and I still wondered just how equitable the GWC would be in the healthcare "business".

Cart continued to listen attentively, but I guess I tuned out the remainder of the physicians' report. I couldn't help but think of the obvious widespread problems in this country regarding healthcare. It was no secret that industrially advanced nations like the United States and Great Britain still offered the best, most up to-date medical care. Not to mention that typically, those with the money got the better services. And on top of that, the ugly monsters called racism and social class were still alive and well. A rich white person had connections, and could still get what ever he, or she wanted with few complications—organ transplants, successfully proven AIDS fighting drugs, extensive spinal-cord injury therapy—just to name a few. How well could the Greater World Council really level the playing field?

Next, the GWC Economic Committee was given front and center stage. They too started out with a history of why the economy of individual countries and nations faltered. The United States was repeatedly blamed for allowing partisan politics to create tremendous waste of tax dollars, and loss of respect as a world leader. The U.S. was ridiculed for expensive and lengthily inquiries like the investigations into former Bill Clinton's sexual activities, and extra-marital affairs. When America was the leading world power in economic development the national and international impact of these investigations, along with drastic shifts in the stock market, company mergers, and downsizing created an unfavorable affect that was felt around the globe. Businesses and services provided by computer systems developers, banks, communications operations, department stores, and energy companies were offered as examples depicting smaller companies eaten-up by larger conglomerates of the same. Time and time again as various companies sought to be the biggest, best, and most competitive, jobs were ultimately eliminated.

The average worker was often left scrambling to recover. Losing a job usually didn't mean being able to move onto a comparable position elsewhere. Often it meant taking a lower paying job, when lucky enough to find an alternative. This was especially true for non-whites, over 45. The words "Equal Opportunity" could always be found on a job application, or posted in a well framed statement hanging somewhere in a Human Resources office, or boldly displayed with on-line employment listings from the internet. However, in 2020, race, age, and sex discrimination still permeated hiring practices. It was always hard to prove, but easy to recognize when one was on the receiving end.

The next panel of internationals declared that the GWC's solution to the ever-present problems caused by human inequalities was to eliminate competition on all levels, and in all arenas. Cart and I sat up straight, wide-eyed and hopeful, as we prepared to absorb more of the transmission.

*   *   *   *

Breaktime went by quicker than ever before. My hot turkey platter was actually room temperature slithers of light and dark turkey covered in a liquid that vaguely resembled gravy. The mashed potatoes were mashed in some places, clumped in others. The green beans were nearly raw, although it was announced that they would be steamed and lightly seasoned. Ironically, only the fresh peaches were a welcomed site. I knew they would be good.

Lunch was over and now I was expected to return to the peach grove. A climatically controlled grove of genetically engineered peach trees. None of which was less than 40 feet tall. Each tree produced astronomical amounts of large juicy peaches year round. Besides the nutritional value associated with this particular fruit, its pit was discovered to drastically aid in curing some cancers. The peach pits were grounded and mixed with other cancer fighting agents to create wonder drugs. Harvesting peaches quickly became a global interest.

Global interest, or not, and in spite of Carther's ailing health I was supposed to continue working as usual. I was suppose to pull a basket off the supply rack, return to the sweet smelling trees, and resume my picking. Just like always for the last 2 1/2 years. No matter what, Carther and I still had our credit card debts to work off. But, today was different. Today I couldn't "bite the bullet," and keep on "truck-in." I refused to once again blend in with the stream of fellow pickers adorned in bright orange coveralls and brown cotton work gloves. Today Cart needed me more than ever before. Today we were separated for the first time in our lives!

So full of emotion and determination, I bolted from my normal path. As if in automatic gear my body turned and marched straight for the Head Master's office. This was a bold and desperate move for me, but now there was no turning back. I had to see Cart. They just had to let me be with him. Only a fool would try to run away from the groves, or storm the gate. No matter how our lives had changed, I was no fool. I was still intelligent and sensible. I could talk with reason. I would make the Head Master see the urgency in this situation.

I approached Head Master Bryant Young's pavilion quietly. As expected, I was quickly halted by the guards. They were never reluctant to honor, serve, and protect the establishment. They weren't working off credit cards debts. They were employed by the Greater World Council Security Division. The Security Division had several levels from Inter-Galactic and Nuclear Surveillance, to local community patrol, to lowly armed security guards like the ones that faced me with fierce and threatening looks.

"Stop!"

They growled in unison like perfectly trained seals. My knees buckled. My heart leaped and pounded loudly in my chest.

"I need to see Master Young right away! My husband collapsed in the groves. They took him away!"

I expected to be ridiculed, or admonished. Instead of turning me away, or threatening to have me marked for correction they calmly looked down on me from what must have been six feet-seven inch statures, and firmly directed me to be silent and remain there. Fear and anticipation stiffened my bones like blocks of ice. Movement was out of the question. I was emotionally and physically paralyzed. A third guard approached us quickly. The two watchmen towering over me repeated my plea. To my surprise and relief, the third guard escorted me to the Head Master's front office.

Gloria Newcomer greeted me apprehensively. She knew I had not been summoned, and she didn't like anything happening out of the ordinary. I wasn't sure if I was glad to see her either. Gloria was Native American, and one of the few people of color in a position of some authority, but everyone knew she was the perfect gatekeeper. Gloria had no friends, and formed no allegiances at the orchard. She was efficient and all about business. She didn't engage in conversation unless it was work related. Gloria never put her self in the position to owe anyone a favor, or extend any preferential treatment. In spite of her immediate displeasure in my showing up at her desk, she kept her cool.

I repeated my reason for being there. Her tough exterior seemed to soften. Subtle looks of compassion began to replace her normal frowns and stern manner. Deep down inside, Gloria always remembered she was really one of us. Her position as secretary to the Head Master did not require her to wear orange coveralls like the pickers, but she was there for the same reason—working off heaps of credit card debt. Gloria instructed me to go to the waiting area. Dutifully the guard escorted me there. He watched me quickly scan the small, thickly carpeted room. A well-polished solid mahogany worktable and six plush chairs were neatly stacked against the room's walls. The richly textured furniture was obviously placed there for storage, and not for use. There was no place to sit at the moment. The guard followed on my heels, and retained his staunch demeanor only inches from my side. I could feel him look down on me as if I was some kind of murderous criminal. Someone wasting his time.

Five minutes went by. That was easy. I prayed for strength and mercy. Twenty more minutes dragged by. I had more time to pray, more time to think, more time to feel increased weakness in my legs and pain in my lower back. No matter what, I knew that God would never forsake Cart and me. He never did—not even once during the last 2 1/2 years of picking.

Most importantly, we knew that our children were safe, and had adapted quickly to this New World order. They were all working and in their thirties when Cart and I were assigned as pickers. In the Greater World Council all salaries were greatly reduced from what people had become accustomed to in middle-class America. No one made enough money to bail parents, or other relatives out of credit card debt.

All types of insurance policies were canceled and non-refundable. The Greater World Council's existence was to insure that everyone was cared for and had fulfillment in life. No one retained any individual wealth or assets. Personal bank accounts and investments were liquidated and used to pay off debts. What ever an individual had left over was absorbed by the GWC. This was felt to be morally right because now the GWC universally supported all human needs. Besides, currency was abolished. Those left without enough assets to cover all debts during the transition became debtor workers like Cart and me.

Debtor workers essentially served two purposes: 1) The GWC was very concerned with maintaining a good work ethnic. That collective attitude was paramount to the success of the GWC. Everyone had to basically think on one supportive accord. There's no more effective pressure than peer pressure. Therefore, it was mandated that all debts would be repaid in order that no one could feel that they gained anything without paying for it fully, or working for it; and 2) The Greater World Council well realized that during the transition years to its way of life, large numbers of menial laborers would be needed to perform various tasks to develop and re-develop regions. Truly a concept borrowed from history's countless examples of enslaving people. My own African ancestors were forcibly brought to America for economic reasons. At that time it was the economics of harvesting vast cotton, sugar, and rice fields. History had a way of repeating itself in some form or another.

Credit card debt had reached massive proportions by 2019 when the GWC was formally established. That's why there were so many debtor workers. Thank God, by 2012, banks stopped some of their insane practices, like issuing credit cards to minors and unemployed college students. This removed a temptation that should have never been born in the first place. Elimination of student revolving credit, along with Carther and I constantly showing the kids how not to fall into the same "get now—pay later" trap that snared us, proved to be key in keeping our children out of heavy debt.

In these transition years to full compliance with the Greater World Council, those who did not become debtor workers generally stayed in their current field of work, but were paid in "earned credits". Thus, the new systems of salary and payment were established. Electronic, pocketsize cards were methods of exchange, replacing all forms of currency, and greatly resembling the appearance of credit cards from the past, but provided no ability to purchase now and pay later. The cards were scanned at merchandising centers, and thereby checked for actual earned credits or points to make a purchase. Cards were easily electronically updated, or credited at a person's place of work. This process encompassed the new "payroll" system. Items and services like housing, food, electricity, and healthcare were provided without charge. They were among the necessities of life as outlined by the GWC. For such, care, everyone was taught that they were responsible to work. A strong willingness to work, and to perform a superb job demonstrated acknowledgment and gratitude for what the GWC provided.

Unemployment as we knew it completely disappeared. Welfare had long ago become a "dirty" word. There was always some form of paid work to perform in support of running and maintaining of one's region. Life under the GWC eliminated the need for global competition of any type. The value of all professions was considered equal. The services of a surgeon were equally valued with sanitation workers. Some professions completely disappeared, or were transformed. Investment bankers instantly became obsolete when stocks, currency, and asset portfolios were deemed the "root of all evil."

Working also provided a means to receive perks. The perks were essentially purchased with one's earned credits, or salary. Saving too many credits at a time was considered hoarding, and quickly questioned. Besides, the entire concept of personal long-term savings had become archaic. Things like accent furniture pieces, pets, or gourmet foods—items that were deemed not essential to life—were considered perks, and purchased with earned credits. Perks were effective incentives that kept people happy and feeling as if they were still individuals. Nonetheless, loyalty to the Greater World Council had become a global way of life. That loyalty was paramount above anything else.

Carther and I resolved to the fact that we were responsible for paying back our debts. "Lord forgive us our debts as we forgive our debtors." Forgiving didn't necessarily mean wiping the slate clean without owning-up to our part in this mess. Personal and corporate bankruptcy had been abolished in the year 2015. Now, in 2023, we just never dreamt our fate would come to isolation from family, manual labor, and loss of control over our activities. Who could we blame?

*   *   *   *

"Have a seat, Annie."

He sounded so omnipotent, and controlling. Just like any corporate CEO, this head master had all the right non-verbal gestures and mannerisms to let me know he was in charge. He greeted me with one hand in his pocket, just having released the other in time to display a broad-arm motion to sit where he indicated.

"I understand you left your assigned post without authorization."

"Yes, sir. I need to know how Carther's doing. He became ill this morning and was rushed to the medical center. I just need to know how he is."

I felt myself loosing my grip. My voice quivered. I lost eye contact, and looked down to see my legs shaking. Why did he have to make this so difficult? Don't I have any rights left?

"Yes. I know all about Carther's taking ill."

In his next breath he started sounding off about rules and regulations, and how leaving my assigned post for any reason without permission was grounds to be marked for correction. He went on a ridiculous tangent about keeping order and following rules. He spouted out rhetoric on why the system of 'marks for correction' was devised—calling it a motivator. Of course it was a motivator, punishment, and controller all wrapped in one! Pickers are here to work off debts. No one wants to stay here any longer than he or she has to. No one wants to pick bushel after bushel, year after year, and at any time have their total reduced by some arbitrary amount. An amount that would represent a "proper punishment", a mark for correction. The ancients used whips to force workers into submission. I suppose any undesirable consequence will bring about the same result—surrender to the "powers that be."

"HEAD MASTER YOUNG!"

He looked at me in disbelief. Not only had I interrupted him, I raised my voice too!

"I've approached you out of a sincere and honest desire to simply learn of my husband's condition. I'm not trying to slouch on my work. I'm not expecting anyone to cover my count. I'm still a human being, and my husband of 32 years still matters to me very much. Regardless of our situation as pickers, we can still be respected."

Thank-you, Lord! Suddenly I felt like myself again. Months and months of living and working at the orchard, being told what to do, and when to do it had made me dull to God's power within. I had lost touch with my selfworth. I had to remind myself that God was with me every step of the way. Yes. Cart and I had to face-up to our predicament, and work our way out of this mess, but we've never been alone. God's Holy Spirit still guided us. He always cared!

"Anna Patrice Bethune. You have a lot of nerve confronting me in this manner!"

He paused, and pierced my entire being like a long fiery arrow. The heat of his anger gave me chills. With a deep sigh and long stare he continued.

"Yes, Annie. In your situation I suppose it does take a lot of nerve to be heard. I truly am saddened by Carther's illness, just as I would be concerned about any of the pickers. You must understand that I'm charged with the responsibility to keep order and production at all times in this facility. Feelings really can't enter into my job, but I'm not callous."

His change in manner, and unexpected revelation completely stunned me. I knew I was still in his office, but suddenly in such a surrealistic mode I felt miles away. It was as if I was removed to some comfortable, cozy place looking in and observing someone else's dilemma. I had finally been heard. I could finally take a deep breath. I exhaled with renewed confidence.

"Annie. I'll make arrangements for you to have an extended stay with Cart. You should remain at his bedside for as long as you like. Carther's in a single room. I'll arrange for an additional bed to be wheeled in for your comfort. He is quite sick, Annie. This is a time you need be together."

I left his office trading one burden for another. The thought of losing Cart was more than I could bear. Yet, I knew that God was still alive and well in this New World order. I knew that his goodness and mercy could not be repressed. I knew he was still in charge.

The rich rules over the poor
And the borrower becomes the lender's slave.

—Proverbs 22:7

THE END

STORY #3:
TURNABOUT

Part I

Mattie's dreadful wailing and frantic pleas could be heard clear across the plantation. The older slave women shook their heads in sadness and pity. They had told her not to get so attached to that boy.

"Masta Cooper bound to sell that youn'in on down to the Buford plantation in Georgia. See'n as though they made some kind of agreement before that child was ever born."

The men folk warned her too.

"We ain't got a chance to have families like white folks do. We's slaves in this land. White folks don't care 'bout us having and caring for our own families. They just want they crops planted and picked. That's how they get richer and richer. The mo' slaves a Masta has, the mo' work can be done. They gonna sell dat boy sure 'nough. He's a big buck right from birth! Likely, they gonna raise him fir breeding mo' big'ins just like his pappy breeded him."

Franklin Lee Cooper had summoned Mattie to bring the boy to a small barn near the stables. The driver from Buford's plantation would be arriving soon and Franklin Cooper was preparing to make the exchange. Franklin Cooper was also waiting for the Markley brothers. They were his overseers and farm hands. Franklin expected them back from town shortly. They were only sent to pick up supplies.

Tom and Joseph Markley were loyal to the Coopers for taking them in when their home burned down and their parents were killed in the blaze. That was 14 years ago. The brothers, now 22 and 24 years old, had learned the ins and outs of tobacco farming, curing, and selling. They had also become invaluable to Franklin when it came to keeping the slaves in line. The brothers were rough on them at times, but Franklin felt that's what it took to keep slaves under control. He usually let the Markley's handle discipline issues. The brothers would be back in an hour or two to deal with the new slaves coming in from old man Buford's plantation. He began to quickly realize how much he could use their "expertise" at the moment.

Franklin Lee Cooper could not believe his eyes, or ears. He never anticipated this scene in the tobacco barn. Mattie was down on her knees with the baby clutched in her arms. Tears and snot running down her face like a woman purely insane. The shoulders of her tattered plain cotton dress ripped instantly when she struggled and yanked away from his grasp. Her otherwise bare feet were wrapped in once discarded strips of old burlap sackcloth; the material from cloth bags flour was sold in. The strips of available cloth were Mattie's meager attempt to provide some foot covering since shoes or boots were usually not given to slaves. The late March snow-stained ground left the strips soaking wet, and now they began to unravel with her every move.

"No Masta Cooper. Please, please sir. Don't take my youn'in from me. He's my only child. I do what ever you say, just please don't send my baby away. We's here in North Carolina. I'll never see him again if'in you send him so far away. Please sir. I wants to be his mammy. He's my flesh and blood. Please sir, please!"

Mattie tearfully screamed and hollered repeatedly. The baby's wailing ascended in unison with his mother's. This was all nonsense to Cooper. He hadn't planned on any trouble from Mattie. He had once thought of her as his favorite, and most obedient gal. Any night he took her for himself, or made her available to his gentlemen friends she was never a problem.

That's partly why he arranged for Mattie to be paired up with that breeding buck on loan from old man Buford. She was obedient and a good size gal for 15 years of age. That buck was bigger than a bull. They were bound to have big healthy offspring for farm labor, or breeding. And from the looks of their youn'in all balled up in Mattie's arms, he was bigger than most children twice his age.

Besides, a deal is a deal. Franklin Cooper recently purchased 6 additional acres that needed clearing for tobacco planting. He was ready to hand over the year-old slave child in exchange for 3 good field slaves. His plan was to put them to work as soon as the late frost cleared. Jeremy Buford planned on raising the boy to do some stable work, but mainly to use him as a breeder—if he proved to be big and strong like his pappy. Franklin had also thrown in $400 to sweeten the deal.

"No crazy nigga woman is gonna stand in my way! Mattie! So help me God. I'm gonna put stripes on your back if you don't stop this madness. You and that picanninney ain't nothing but my property. You do as I say!"

Franklin Cooper had never taken the whip across Mattie's back and he never let anyone else do it either. However, today was about to be the exception.

Rose listened to the ruckus from the tobacco barn for at least a half-hour. She was disgusted that her husband even entertained the idea of reasoning with Mattie. She was fed up with everything concerning Mattie. Rose had spent a growing accumulation of hours alone in her bed at night waiting for her husband to come to her side, to desire her, to take her in his arms. Yet, time and time again, he took his pleasures with those slave girls—Mattie in particular.

Rose believed that having slaves and doing as one pleased with them was a white man's right. Afterall, she reasoned, God must want it that way. Slavery was happening all around them, and good white folks prospered. Rose felt that she and Franklin were good Christian people too. She believed they fed and clothed their slaves better than most white folks did.

Rose thought back to being gravely ill with pneumonia in 1826, just last winter. She relived the anguish of not being able to perform her "wifely duties". She was 28 years old and on the verge of death. Franklin made certain she was well cared for. He ordered her bed linen and gowns changed daily. He had additional down pillows stitched with elaborate embroidery and stuffed with extra feathers in order that she would have something pretty to look at, and to prop her up in bed when she was too weak to sit up on her own. The house slaves were kept on alert, and never allowed to leave her alone, not for one minute. At night, a young slave girl about eight years of age laid across the foot of Rose's bed to keep Rose's feet warm, and to make certain the covers stayed on her all through the night. When the girl did not perform her tasks satisfactorily she was whipped the next morning.

To Rose, when she took ill it seemed God-sent that Franklin could satisfy his manly needs with those slaves. But now that she was well and strong again she could resume her affections towards him. Yet, he didn't seem to notice. She felt totally alone and discarded.

Repeatedly Rose felt her heart screaming, 'Franklin keeps tak'in those nigger gals to himself, especially that Mattie! This just ain't right. This can't be what God had in mind for good Christian people like Franklin and me. Somehow, someway, I'm gonna stop this.' Rose painfully admitted that she grew to recognize the gleam in Franklin's eyes, the evidence of lust leaping in his groin when he was about to summon Mattie to the tobacco barn.

Franklin was careful never to bring Mattie into the main house, nor would he ever go over to the dismal slave quarters. But, in the tobacco barn, in a closed-in side room, he had a fireplace and wooden floor built. He kept a big oak bed with clean sheets and covers on it. In her mind Rose replayed Franklin's words making it clear to her that she was never to go into that barn......

"Now Rose, the tobacco barn is no place I <u>ever</u> want you trampling in. The work's all done by who I say does it. I can't have you gett'in sick again. The doctor says you gotta keep your lungs clear. That's why I don't even want you near that barn. You're delicate and a fine white woman. I'm your husband and I'll keep you from harm. Now I know years past you were frett'in that we didn't have any children. However, I see that's best now. You don't need that strain on yourself. You do as I say, and stay away from the tobacco barn."

Rose well understood the "work" of the tobacco barn. During the day, the Markley brothers and designated slaves tended to the tobacco curing. At night, Franklin alone or with gentleman guests would do as they wished with the slave girls.

Rose could no longer ignore the outburst. "Surely the whole plantation must be aware of it by now," she murmured. She bolted from her room quicker than March wind gusts tossed about loose twigs. Before she knew it, she had hustled from her plush bedroom to the doorway of the tobacco barn, nearly 70 yards away. Now she could witness the source of the commotion. Rose immediately surveyed Franklin's twisted facial expression as it seemed to escalate from great annoyance to sheer rage. His body appeared ridged and strangely mechanical as he moved in closer to the screaming slaves now crouched down in a corner near the barn entrance. The sweet smell of once cured tobacco leaves painted the air all around them.

Suddenly, Mattie leaped from her crouched position with her screaming baby firmly pressed to her chest, locked in place by her unfolded arms. She strategically used her slightly extended elbows to plow pass Franklin Cooper. Mattie had no idea her mistress was standing in the doorway until their eyes met. Rose made an attempt to push Mattie down as she sprinted towards the doorway. Mattie's quickened momentum and obvious rush of adrenaline gave her the fierce strength to pound Rose with a solid kick to her abdomen as she vaulted several inches off the ground and propelled herself and her precious bundle through the doorway.

Mattie's fear kept her afoot and oblivious to the cold. The air suddenly took on a new odor. It smelled of freedom. Mattie knew she had only one thing left to do—keep running. It was cold, damp and not quite dusk. White men with guns in their arms and bloodhounds by their sides would surely come after them soon. She wasn't certain when she'd ever-quiet little Jo-Jo. Could they even find a place to hide? She resolved to run as far and for as long as she could. She would not acknowledge the frost laidened ground beneath her now bare feet.

Jo-Jo was wrapped in an old partially moth eaten woolen blanket her baby sister once used. Mattie could barely remember her sister or her mother and father. They were sold off long ago. But the older slave women made a promise to her mother to pass on the blanket as something to think of them by. Growing up Mattie often wrapped the blanket around her shoulders, or rubbed it against her cheeks. She sometimes smiled and dreamt of a different life. Most times she cried and agonized over her situation. Now the blanket comforted the one thing that made her life worthwhile, her Jo-Jo.

Still running and strangely renewed, Mattie knew she would be killed for her sampling of freedom. Jo-Jo would never remember her, and probably never know his father. At least the slaves she now left behind could pass on her story, a story of determination and a few brief moments of freedom.

Everything happened so quickly in the tobacco barn. Franklin Cooper watched with disbelieve as his wife fell down to the dirt floor. He cursed Mattie furiously as he ran over to Rose.

"Don't touch me," Rose screamed angrily as she clutched her stomach.

Franklin chose to ignore his wife's demand and attempted to pull her to her feet. To his dismay, Rose slapped him across his face. The slap was such a forceful and deliberate swing that it caused her to tilt over to one side. Her body spread out even further across the cold, dirty barn floor.

"You fool," Rose blurted.

Franklin Cooper was now responding to his second shock of the day—defiance from his dutiful wife. His face was easy to read. Rose interpreted his every thought. While slowly pulling herself upright and then gradually to her feet, she took this opportunity to sound off on him.

"Franklin Lee Cooper! You have lost control and power around here. Your fool'in with this slave gal has caused me great harm. You may have forgotten about me in some ways, but I'm still the mistress of this plantation and no slave is gonna attack me and live. I demand that you kill that Mattie <u>and</u> her miserable child. Shoot'em, hang'em—whatever! They must die for this outrage!"

Franklin looked over at his dissolved wife—his face still tingled from the sting of her slap. He thought of a dozen responses, but none were more prominent than proving her wrong and preserving his authority.

Unknowingly to the Coopers the scene outside the tobacco barn had changed dramatically. Several house and field slaves had ventured away from their assigned areas. From a few feet away some were attempting to peer in the barn's entrance to see what was going on. Most could clearly hear the boisterous exchange between the Coopers.

The Markley brothers rode up in their wagon taking in the odd scene as they approached the tobacco barn. With his rifle in hand, Tom, the younger brother jumped out of the wagon while it was still in motion. Running across the yard he pushed aside the few slaves who dared to stand in his path. He steam-rolled into the tobacco barn just in time to observe Franklin Cooper attempt to respond to his wife. Now with an audience, Cooper felt compelled to boldly announce what had occurred.

"Damn-it Tom! There's been big trouble 'round here while you and Joseph were gone. That Mattie gal took her youn'in and ran off. Before leav'in for the woods she kicked my beloved Rose and knocked her to the ground. All for no reason. She knew we was taken that boy today. She knows that's how it is. That Mattie has to be punished. She has to be an example. We don't want any uprising 'round here! We gonna catch'em and kill'em <u>both</u> so as the rest of the slaves can clearly see I mean to severely punish any one of them that defies the law."

Franklin Cooper swabbed his coat sleeve across his mouth to wipe away spittle than drained from his angry words. He felt in charge. Warning shots from Joseph's rifle pushed the stunned slaves into a huddle away from the tobacco barn. Tom was the first to look out and see his brother approaching. Tom and Franklin exited the barn to join Joseph and to observe the results of his gunfire. Standing outside of the tobacco barn in the late afternoon chill of a mild March frost, the three white men quickly joined together to formulate a plan of action. All 36 slaves were frozen in their positions as Rose took in the whole scene from her new vantage point, leaning against an exterior wall of the barn.

Franklin ordered Tom and Joseph to move the field slaves back to their quarters. His two trusted house slaves were instructed to take Mrs. Cooper back to the house and comfort her. All obeyed as commanded.

Franklin then sent Tom to their closest neighbors, the Wisners, a family of vegetable farmers. They were poor and always grateful for the little help the Coopers were willing to extend to them. For Franklin it was always just enough help to remind the family that they should remain "good" white people and make themselves available when called on. To the family, any assistance from Franklin Cooper added to their survival. They were loyal to the cause.

From the moment Mattie and Jo-Jo entered the woods they were not alone. Gabe well remembered every hope and dream Mattie had ever uttered about keeping their baby. He knew she would be crazy enough, determined enough to have life her way. Despite his fearful reluctance, Gabe became caught-up in the notion of being free and in control.

He wasn't sure how it happened. Like Mattie, he too had learned to ignore his own feelings and do as the slave master commanded. His life as a breeder was so ambiguous. Physically, he had the benefit of sexual activity, yet emotionally there was total emptiness. He was a slave forced to impregnate other slaves for the purpose of breeding more slaves. With each female the slave masters gave him he knew what to expect. Some came willingly to get it over with, and others would fight him off—even to the point of a severe lashing from the master's whip if that's what it took.

Gabe learned to keep his emotions well detached. In order to survive he had to think of himself as just another farm animal, just another creature doing as he was forced to. Disobedience would mean brutal consequences. Whippings, castration, or hanging were methods of punishment commonly used by the slave masters to instill fear in the heart of any slave, thereby controlling groups of slaves. Slaves had limited access to weapons due to their masters' fear of retaliation. Most were fed far less than adequate food. On many plantations like the Cooper's, slaves lived in poorly structured cabins with no windows and full of cracks that invited cold air in. Slaves were given sub-standard clothing year-round and were usually barefoot during the warmer and sometimes colder months.

Gabe was nearly 15 years old before he even received his first pair of pants. Growing up the boys and girls were given only long white shirts to wear and no underwear. The single garment served as minimal covering for their youthful bodies. This was yet another means of control. It was a way to reinforce a slave master's control over every aspect of a slave's life. Psychologically it served to manifest that slaves "deserved" only minor consideration—leaving a slave child to grow up feeling like less than a whole person.

When Mattie was brought to him he was 20 years old and well indoctrinated into the slave existence. Gabe had no idea he would grow to plan for a better life. He gleaned a spirit of hope from her. He liked to hear Mattie's stories, her memories of her parents. He liked knowing she began to care about him, and to his amazement he began to care about her. Together they created feelings they had never shared with anyone else. Together they created their precious Jo-Jo.

Gabe listened as Mattie and Jo-Jo charged closer. He reflected on the earlier commotion down at the tobacco barn and how he went into action. He knew the Markley brothers were away and that would be his only time to gather what was needed. Gabe had gone into their cabin and took warm clothing, blankets, boots, some dried meat, two rifles and all the ammunition he could find. He never thought of turning back. He was consumed with thoughts of Mattie and Jo-Jo. Yet, the nagging possibility of death pulled at his conscience.

Now dusk, and in the temporary sanctuary of the thick woods, Gabe ran towards Mattie and Jo-Jo. Mattie's emotions peaked when she saw Gabe. 'Could her dreams really come true', she wondered? She and Jo-Jo fell into Gabe's strong waiting arms. They were together as planned.

"We's free Gabe. We's free now!" Mattie cried out vehemently.

"No time for talk'in Mattie. We gotta get you both warm and quiet Jo-Jo. We ain't free 'til we's far away from here."

Mattie loved Gabe's practicality. It's what kept her sane and hopefully would keep them all alive. Right there under a thicket of evergreens and the watchful eye of what appeared to be an old owl, Mattie began her transformation. First, they wrapped Jo-Jo in a triple thick blanket. Gabe held him close to his body and softly hummed to him. Jo-Jo's screams turned into whimpers. Mattie removed her wet, tattered dress and replaced it with warm, dry clothes "courtesy" of the Markley brothers. The two flannel shirts, wool socks and coveralls felt like a mother's protective embrace. But the heavy boots proved to be her greatest comfort. They provided a shield of warmth those strips of burlap sackcloth could never achieve. Before wrapping up in a long woolen coat and knit hat,

Mattie partially unbuttoned her shirts and put the bundled whim-
pering baby to her breast. Gabe used part of a bed sheet to wrap
around Jo-Jo and Mattie, literally tying the baby to her. Mattie's
body gave Jo-Jo additional warmth and the comfort of suckling as
they traveled through the frigid dark night.

Gabe looked down to survey his beloved Mattie and Jo-Jo. For
the first time in his life he knew the meaning of family. He was not
just another farm animal. He was a man with feelings like any man.
He wanted to protect and guide his family. Yet, he lived in a world,
at a time that saw him only as a slave—property to be manipulated
at will. In spite of their odds, Gabe was determined to keep them
free.

"Let's get mov'in, Mattie. If'n we stay here much longer we
gonna hear them bark'in hounds and all of Massa Cooper's posse."

"I knows you right Gabe. I know. I jus' want you to hear me
again. I still mean what I told you before. No matter what happens
we gonna either be together in life, or we gonna be together in
death. I loves you Gabe. Nobody gonna take that from me."

He softly kissed her cold, tear stained cheek, and gently stroked
her chin as he had done so many times before back in his old cabin.
They headed for the safety and seclusion of the nearby mountains.

Gabe had well memorized the hidden path to freedom long ago
told to him by a dying slave who had fled, but was captured way up
north where he had become a free man. That slave master and his

hired posse brought the runaway slave back to their plantation. They tied him to a fence, and whipped him nearly to death, forcing the slaves of every age to witness the punishment. For several days after that he lay in bed semiconscious and burning with fever. The slaves did what they could to care for him. Eventually his wounds became infected and he died. It was then that Gabe decided freedom would never be worth the risk. A risk he never intended to take until Mattie came into his life. She transformed his fear into a determination to live a better life—a life of freedom.

Back at the slave quarters the men and women talked of Mattie's and Gabe's run for freedom. They commented on how Joseph Markley wasted no time finding out if Mattie ran off alone. Their dialogue described how Joseph feverishly took an account of all the slaves before they were allowed back in the cabins. When he discovered Gabe was missing, Joseph seemed to be down right pleased.

One old woman stated, "Ain't nothing worse than chas'in down a slave, but when a man gets pure pleasure from it, it all becomes a diff'rent kinda evil. That Joseph Markley is gonna make big sport of this here track'in."

Most of the other slaves nodded in agreement. Some felt running away was useless. 'Afterall, life was hard enough. Why go run'in off in the late March frost with a youn'in in your arms,' they reasoned. Others imagined a sense of freedom through Gabe and Mattie. Just knowing they defied Franklin Cooper's plan was encouragement. Some seemed to daydream that maybe one day they too would make a run for freedom.

Tom Markley and two young hired hands from the Wisner farm were well armed and left behind to mind the plantation. Under the circumstances and with the hour nearing 7:00 o'clock, the slaves had been ordered to remain in their cabins. Guard dogs were strategically placed outdoors ready to announce any movement. Tom watched intently as his brother and Franklin Cooper took charge of the posse. Four adult men and two adolescent boys came enthusiastically from the Wisner family. They listened steadfastly as Franklin bellowed his directions, sounding like a retired soldier anxious to return to action.

"Listen-up men! Now I know it's start'in to get dark, but we gotta tail them runaways before they get deep in the mountains. If they do, we may never catch'em. Too often the mountain folks help our slaves hide and get away. They don't have large farms to tend like we do. They don't always value the necessity for slave labor. Therefore, we gotta start tracking them now. I trust you brought provisions along. One chilly night in the woods surely won't kill ya! I'm look'in to yank back that crazy Mattie, her thieve'in accomplice Gabe, and I still plan on sending that wailing picanninney down to Old man Buford. We gonna try to catch Mattie and Gabe alive and bring'em back for execution. But if necessary, shoot to kill! Ain't no slaves gonna upset my plans. Alright men, pick up your gear and lets head out!"

Franklin Cooper had just given the boldest speech he'd ever uttered in his 39 years of life. He would not have it said that slaves got away from him. He wanted his property back. Franklin Cooper was the first to mount a steed. His heart beat wildly with anger and a seething desire for revenge. First things first. He'd settle the matter with the slaves and then deal with Rose. He grinned maliciously thinking of her insurrection. Franklin concluded that she too had to be reminded of her place in his life.

Now a few miles away from the posse scene, Jo-Jo had fallen asleep securely hidden, warm and strapped to his mother's belly, close to her nourishing breast. On the outside, the forest temperature was dropping and the air felt icy. But, on the inside, the warmth of family was woven throughout their souls. Their bond was fortified. No matter what happened next they would live or die as a unit. Gabe, Mattie and Jo-Jo felt each other's love as they continued their trek to freedom.

"Look on up there Mattie, Gabe's hushed tone instructed."

"I'm look'in Gabe, but I don't see noth'in but a whisper of the moon. Looks like a few strands of silver-white hair banded together. It's just the new moon com'in on and a few stars start'in to shine up."

"No Mattie, not the moon. Look on over at that old owl. I took notice of him when I first came in the woods. I swear he's been following us."

Mattie kept silent, seeming to wait for further explanation. Gabe was too pensive to respond. He thought more about that same grandfatherly looking owl peering down at them. It's eyes appeared larger and brighter than any other spotted owl he'd ever seen. Maybe it was the darkness of the thick woods, or his own nervousness, but to Gabe the owl seemed to be following them, now more closely than before. He thought of shooting it, but couldn't take the chance of being heard by their trackers. He thought of hurling rocks up at it, but didn't want the bird's noisy reaction to bring attention to them either. There was nothing to do but watch it as it watched them.

"Gotta take just a moment to rest my back Gabe, Mattie exhaled from physical exhaustion." "Can we's stop over there at them rocks, she pleaded softly?"

"Mattie we's jus a little ways from the stream and the entrance to a mountain cave. The way in is pretty well hidden, but I know the markings. In there we'll switch Jo-Jo to me and then I'll carry him. We gonna walk partway through the cave and end up on another side of the mountain. Near there is another cave we can hide in and rest for a little while. But we gonna have to walk all night to stay ahead of that posse and keep'em off our track."

Mattie gently squeezed her man's hand to signal her agreement with his wishes. His reassuring hug was just the inspiration she needed to infuse waning strength. The crackling crickets, moaning toads and the strangely persistent owl seemed to be their only witnesses.

The couple was startled to attention by the sudden breakthrough sounds of excitedly barking hounds and the faint clicks of horses' hoofs.

"Oh no Gabe! We can hear them already. They's too close!" Mattie's frantic whispers propelled Gabe into sudden action.

He hurriedly announced, "Mattie we don't stand a chance if'in we don't cross that stream long before the posse. We's just a quarter mile away. We's gotta run Mattie. We's gotta run hard."

Mattie's only response was to quicken her pace and run alongside him. She silently thanked God that Jo-Jo remained quiet, close and warm, attached to her belly. He never even flinched.

The stream seemed a lifetime away—somewhere buried deep in the molasses colored night. Trampling over stones and loose tree bark flanked by moss, they ran the rocky ground to freedom.

Gabe finally realized that old owl was hopping from tree to tree, just a few feet ahead of them and always in easy hearing range. It made normal hooting sounds, nothing that would be audibly unusual to their trackers. Gabe developed an overwhelming sense that the owl was leading them to safety, not just following along. Humbly he pondered—'Was it an angel in disguise? Angels like the white folks talked about?'

With strained and panting breath Gabe cautiously exclaimed, "We made it to the water Mattie! The water will break our scent some and confuse them ole dogs. Massa Cooper will lead the posse onto the mountain trail. They won't know we's cut across and gone on in that hidden cave over yonder. We's just at the clearing next to the stream.

Their moment of triumph was stifled by the immediate intrusion of Franklin Cooper and Joseph Markley. The still and pristine clearing was suddenly overcome with warning shots from blasting rifles. The two trackers were the first to surprise their prey, silently coming up beside them from the east of the stream. Gabe and Mattie frozen in their steps clung to each other, squeezing their offspring between them. Jo-Jo cried out.

"Over here men! We got'em sure as trapped hogs in a pen!" Franklin Cooper burst out with shear glee.

Luminous lanterns could now be seen peering through the thick dark woods. They were accompanied by horses lead by rowdy villainous predators and their canine companions, once cautioned to be silent, now loudly barking. They were all coming for their prey.

Out of the frosty dark sky a great illumination extended from a tall evergreen. The light became blinding as it cut through the atmosphere and encircled the trapped runaway slaves. The mysterious light quickly extended itself to Franklin Cooper and Joseph Markley. The two stunned white men shot at the light's source, the old spotted owl, now vaguely detectable through the brilliance. The approaching posse was mutually amazed and frightened. They gasped with disbelieve and awe watching the strange illumination swallow up the runaway slaves, Franklin Cooper, and Joseph Markley. The four adults and concealed infant completely vanished before their eyes.

Part II

"Tyrone. Tyrone Curry! They're here! They're here—safe and sound. Come on Doc, where are you?"

Dr. Tyrone Curry repeatedly played his friend and colleague's frantic but jubilant announcement. For nearly an hour the taped-recorded message echoed throughout his tiny, yet adequate apartment.

In solitude, he murmured back to the voice mail message, "Twenty-eight long years I've nursed this project and waited for just the right moment to pluck a sampling of slaves and slave masters from their historical existence—and now….."

"Bleep." "Bleep."

"Who is it!" Tyrone screamed through his front door, the only physical separation between himself and the rest of the world.

"It's me Ty. It's Maleek Bennett. I left you a message hours ago. Everyone is looking for you. What's going on? Are you alright?"

"Go away Maleek. I can't see you now. I can't see anyone."

"What the hell do you mean, man! What's with this 'can't see anybody crap'." Maleek could barely believe he was listening to his long time friend and trusted confidant.

"Ty, either you open this door like you have good sense, or I'm gonna break it down like a madman. What's it gonna be?"

Slowly, with minimal effort Tyrone opened the door to his apartment.

"What's wrong with you Ty? You look a mess. What happened?"

Maleek was visibly stunned by his friend's shabby and bazaar appearance. Looking him over head to toe Maleek couldn't fathom that Tyrone Curry was the same man he worked side by side with at the Institute.

"Ty. Man, I just saw you no more than 24 hours ago. You were fine. What's going on now?"

Both men stood at the doorway, sizing each other up. Tyrone motioned for Maleek to come in and then gently closed the door. Maleek followed Tyrone's non-verbal cues and suddenly found himself in the center of chaos.

A tall bookshelf once home to meticulously organized periodicals, textbooks and memorabilia now lay flat on the floor, face down with its contents scattered about the wood-tiled floor. Wall paintings of proud ancient African Kings and Queens that previously looked down on any visitor had been tossed about the room, discarded like trash in an inner-city subway station.

"Did someone break in and attack you, Ty?"

"No. No. I'm the only perpetrator here."

"Ty. Look at you! Your hair is matted. Looks like it hasn't been picked out in weeks. I see drool dried up all around your mouth and this get-up you're wearing is insane. You'd better explain yourself."

Tyrone looked down at his clothing for the first time and realized he had put on nearly every sweater he owned. Underneath he wore a thick black turtleneck shirt. A pair of pants needing to be hemmed flopped along his long narrow legs. His hands were covered with leather gloves. His feet were bulging and appeared to be double or triple socked. Ty had topped off his strange ensemble with a wide winter scarf that would better serve as a shawl.

Tyrone Curry stared back at his friend showing humility laced with fear. Through teary eyes he begged, "Sit down Maleek. Sit anywhere. Please hear me out."

Maleek found himself adjacent to the livingroom sofa. He mindfully brushed away broken glass and odd debris in order to satisfy a safe place to sit. Tyrone did likewise with a matching ottoman as he prepared to sit across from his friend.

Tyrone sheepishly asked his first question, "Do you remember our first day at the Institute?"

Maleek paused silently, knowing that he and his good friend recounted the events of their first day together many times. It seemed unnecessary to bring it up now, but following along was the only way to get to the root of Tyrone's desperate predicament.

"Sure I do, Ty. We were completing the employment orientation and meeting the evening staff when the research lab exploded and rocked the whole building! The scene was just like something from a disaster flick."

"Yes. Yes, Maleek, but do you remember how we felt heroic and started helping the staff clear out of the building. You found some humor in all that mess. You called us Bio-engineers by day and super heroes by night!"

"Yeah. Yeah, Ty. Hey, we've been partners ever since. But what's going on now?" Maleek heard himself pleading for an explanation.

"Maleek, do you remember how we treated them? How we ignored saving the Greenlees? We didn't even try to help them even though they were easiest for us to reach. We just acted like everyone else. We prioritized those people right out of existence."

"Oh, come on Ty! I can't believe you're bringing that up after all these years. And after our time travel project too! The law is clear and correct. Greenlees are to be separated from the rest of society.

They are not citizens of the world. They are biological mistakes. They are expendable. You know there's always a few of them housed in the lab for experimental purposes, or secured for manual labor. That's all they're good for. Tyrone <u>you</u> have legitimately led the belief that there's no room for a new race of people in the world. You well realize that the evolution of the human species developed over many millennia. The natural combinations of races, geographic location and regional climate created various groups of people around the globe. That's all understood and accepted now. The world, most especially this part of it—the North American continent—has finally reached a multicultural existence fueled by the successful social and economic blending. Like I said, there's no room for a new race of people."

"Maleek don't you see that the Greenlees whole existence is a fluke that scientists like you and I created! We answered the demand for genetically improved intelligence and the elimination of diseases. We had no idea that our tampering would so erroneously and permanently effect the genes of skin and eye pigmentation for those who did not respond favorably to our so-called improvements. We never understood that our apple-green-skinned and green eyed *mistakes* would live on to propagate and establish an existence in the evolutionary chain."

"Science has to incorporate a few stumbling blocks at times, Tyrone."

Maleek's smug response was more than adequate for him, but unnerved his troubled friend. Tyrone's explosive reaction propelled him to his feet from his perch on the wheeled ottoman.

"A FEW STUMBLING BLOCKS!! You want to minimize the existence, the creation of the Greenlees as a few stumbling blocks!"

"Yes Tyrone. Yes I do. And you used to when you were of sound mine."

"Oh Maleek, my mind has never been more sound. I clearly realize that we're the ones who have systematically placed stumbling blocks in the Greenlees way. We've segregated them into specific living areas. We only allow their children to receive a minimal education—just enough knowledge to suitably serve us. They receive the worst food and poorest medical care. We've prevented them from getting life's stimulation."

"Stimulation! Oh come on Tyrone. Man, they don't have the mental or physical capacity to be productive and contribute to society. It's not only that. They look weird with their apple-green skin and eyes. Their colorless hair is just too strange to take seriously. They don't even sound like us when they speak. How much stimulation do they need to learn the language? And I swear everyone of them smells funny!"

"What about those with rare latent symptoms Maleek? Do you still think they should be made to live as the Greenlees do? Will they be subject to our project too—even if they developed the disorder later in life?"

"Ty, a Greenlee is a Greenlee, at birth, middle age or whenever. We're just the scientists here. Global legislators okayed our project to study the methodology of slavery in colonial America with the intent to apply what we learn to our current Greenlee problem. You know that our goal has always been to control *every* member of the Greenlee population, whether they are confirmed at birth or realized at a later time. These beings are of no consequence. Organized enslavement is the best solution to the problem. Under our control they can provide needed manual labor and free up the rest of society to pursue proper goals. It's designed to be a workable solution."

Tyrone appeared more dazed than ever before as he listened to the man he called his best friend. His world continued to cave in as he absorbed those stale words once again confirming what he had worked so hard to achieve and now was so ashamed of.

"Please Maleek. Please don't repeat what I already know. I'm well aware of the time and effort that has gone into snatching that sample of slaves and slave masters across time."

"Are you worried about the time travelers, Ty? Let me remind you. After we glean all the information we need from them. After we learn first hand all there is to learn about the intricate methodologies of slavery, they will be rehabilitated. We'll bring them up to speed with the New World and they'll live out their lives in this time. We'll free their minds, so to speak. Their quality of life will dramatically improve. No harm, no foul!"

Looking puzzled by his friend's ease in justifying their quest to enslave the Greenlees, Tyrone saw a mirror image of what used to be him, until just a day ago. Now terribly fatigued, Tyrone spoke softly with grave reverence.

"I once zealously felt as you do Maleek. Your explanation had been quite suitable for me. But that was when I felt in control. That was before my life changed."

The need for words had been exhausted. Tyrone quietly took three broad steps back from his friend and gradually disrobed. First he peeled away his sweaters, dropping them one-by-one to the floor. His stiff, robotic motions seemed to mimic an apprehensive first-time stripper.

Next, he removed the leather gloves. Maleek immediately developed an alarming frown. He leaned forward, taking in the first glimpse of Tyrone's once cinnamon-colored hands, now cloaked with a brilliant green hue. Tyrone proceeded to remove the last bit of clothing that concealed his shameful torso. He removed his turtle neck shirt and revealed his new green skin.

"Oh my God, Tyrone. You're a Greenlee! How could this be? You're years past the latency symptoms. Is this some kind of trick?"

"It's probably just a matter of days before my face, eyes and hair make the transformation. I'll become an outcast, an undesirable. Someone you and the rest of the world will enslave. Once a predator and now the prey. What a painful turnabout!"

Tyrone's agonizing sarcasm attacked the numbness in the air. Maleek felt powerless too as he sadly observed his long time friend and colleague.

"My transformation will be called a tragedy Maleek, but it will never stop the project the Institute has spent decades developing. Are you prepared Maleek? Are you really prepared to systematically perpetuate hate and prejudice? Will Greenlee woman be abused and victimized as Mattie and thousands of other slave women experienced? Are you ready to snatch Greenlee babies from their mother's arms? Didn't you see enough through the 'wise' owl's eyes? Are you really ready to be a slave master—a Tom or Joseph Markley—a Franklin Lee Cooper?"

"Ty, I'll help you any way I can. I'll keep you hidden. No one will ever have to know. But I'm not ready to be a revolutionary like some of our ancestors. I'm no Martin, or Malcolm or Mandela."

"No, Maleek but now I have to be. The tables have turned for me. I'm no longer a part of this evenly blended world. I'm a Greenlee."

The questions swelled in their hearts. How could they expect to move forward now by looking back, by relying on the hatred and fear they witnessed through the owl's eyes? Is turnabout fair play? Each man looked at the other. Both feeling instantly changed. Both feeling a sorrow and compassion for a situation neither thought would ever effect them personally. Eventually, their slow forming smiles pierced the silence that divided them. Despite the odds, they understood a new plan of action had to be evoked. Only time would tell.

THE BEGINNING

0-595-25028-9